TINA LOUISE
ILLUSTRATED BY OLIVER CORWIN
WHEN I
GROW UP

ABRAMS BOOKS FOR YOUNG READERS
NEW YORK

I can be an architect!

If a firefly can glow in the dark,

If an ant can leave its hill to explore,

If a seal can swim deep
underwater,

I can be a scuba diver!

If a chameleon can change its color,

If a dog can help a person cross the street,

If an elephant can
shake hands
with its trunk,

If a tiger can show its young how to hunt,

If a bird can fly high in the sky,

If a cheetah can run
seventy miles an hour,

I can be an Olympic athlete.

If a male sea horse can give birth,

If a caterpillar can turn
into a butterfly,

when I
GROW UP,
I can be anything I want!

To the children of P.S. 59, who have kept a smile in my heart.
To children all over the world. And to my daughter, Caprice, who I enjoyed reading to,
singing to, and laughing with.
—T. L.

For my grandparents
—O. C.

Acknowledgments

I want to thank and acknowledge Mary Noonan, who loved the idea of this book and now resides in Heaven; my publisher, Howard Reeves, for appreciating the concept immediately; the talented Oliver Corwin; the oh-so-creative Chad Beckerman; George Vellonakis, the godfather of this book; my daughter, Caprice Crane, for constant love and support; Leslie Zackman, former principal of P.S. 59; Regina Migdal, teacher at P.S. 59 and dear friend; and Terrence Schley. Thank you all for your encouragement and help. And lastly, thanks to the New York Public Library. —T. L.

Author's Note

When I Grow Up is a book to empower children to be whoever they want to be and to show them the many possibilities open to them.

I am a school volunteer and I love it. I've been a Learning Leader for eleven years. It's amazing even to me how this contribution has taken over my heart and life and given me such pleasure. I've worked with several children each year, and at the end of each year I have mixed emotions. I'm sad the year is over, but happy I've helped a child to read. Books, art, and music civilize us as a society.

Enabling a child to read has meant so much to me. The children I've worked with have enriched my life enormously, and hopefully their learning experience has expanded.

Teaching children the skill of reading and a love for the written word is important because this will remain with them throughout their lives. If we can reach children at an early age, I believe it will make a difference. This thought brings me tremendous joy.

Library of Congress Cataloging-in-Publication Data
Tina Louise 1934–
When I Grow Up / by Tina Louise ; illustrated by Oliver Corwin.
p. cm.
Summary: Observing the amazing things that animals can do, a child imagines becoming an architect, a teacher, or an Olympic athlete one day.
ISBN-13: 978-0-8109-3948-6
ISBN-10: 0-8109-3948-7
[1. Occupations—Fiction. 2. Animals—Fiction.] I. Corwin, Oliver 2., ill. II. Title.

PZ7.T498Whe 2007
[E]—dc22
2005035489

Text copyright © 2007 Tina Louise
Illustrations copyright © 2007 Oliver Corwin

Book design by Chad W. Beckerman
Production manager: Alexis Mentor

Published in 2007 by Abrams Books for Young Readers, an imprint of Harry N. Abrams, Inc. All rights reserved. No portion of this book may be reproduced, stored in a retrieval system, or transmitted in any form or by any means, mechanical, electronic, photocopying, recording, or otherwise, without written permission from the publisher.
Printed and bound in Singapore
10 9 8 7 6 5 4 3 2 1

HNA
harry n. abrams, inc.
a subsidiary of La Martinière Groupe
115 West 18th Street
New York, NY 10011
www.hnabooks.com